HOW TO GET TO SAVTA'S FOR

SHABBAT

BY VARDA LIVNEY

BOKER TOV! * *GOOD MORNING

TODAY IS FRIDAY, AND YOU KNOW WHAT THAT MEANS.

TONIGHT IS SHABBAT!

WE'RE GOING TO SAVTA'S, AND FRED IS COMING TO PICK US UP IN AN HOUR. SO...

GET THE BACKPACK!

PACK A CHALLAH!

PACK CANDLES!

PACK GRAPE JUICE!

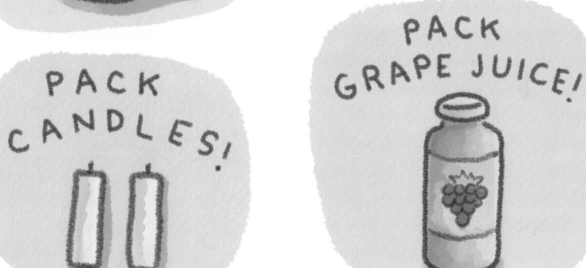

WAIT. WHO'S FRED?

THROUGH

DOWN

THE SLIDE

UP TO THE

MOON

SHABBAT

Published in 2022 by PJ Publishing, an imprint of PJ Library

PJ Publishing creates board books, picture books, chapter books, and graphic novels in multiple languages that represent the diversity of Jewish families today. By sharing Jewish narratives, values, and life events, we help families explore their connections with Jewish life.

Library of Congress Control Number: 2021948808

Designed by Michael Grinley

First Edition
10 9 8 7 6 5 4 3 2 1
0622/B1879/A3
Printed in China